My Name is Mary

The Story of the Mother of Jesus

DENISE SAWYER

Virginia

MY NAME IS MARY: THE STORY OF THE MOTHER OF JESUS
© 2002 by Denise Sawyer

Still Waters Publishers
P.O. Box 403
Dunn Loring, VA 22027

Book design by Sara Patton
Cover design by George Foster
Original cover art by Denise Sawyer
Author photo by Roger Sawyer
Printed in the United States of America

ISBN: 0-9714276-4-X
LCCN: 2001119045

"He leadeth me beside the still waters,
He restoreth my soul."

Psalm: 23:2-3

Dedication

I would like to dedicate this book to my mother, Edna Meyer Jones, who passed away on the day after Thanksgiving, 2001. She was the very first person to read *My Name is Mary,* and her positive reaction and immediate support gave me the courage to share it with others. I will miss her forever.

Aknowledgments

I would like to thank my brother, Darryl Jones, for his wise suggestions and for all that he has taught me over the years. Thank you to Elaine Devine for her early encouragement and continuous support. Thanks also to Susan Kumbera, my father William B. Jones, Jr., our sons David and Michael Sawyer, and to Sarah Lally. I especially want to thank my husband, Roger Sawyer, my principal editor, who has always been there to listen to me and to advise me. I could not have done this without you, and I am grateful for your love and support.

Introduction

When I woke up on Thursday morning of Holy Week, 2001, writing a book about Mary, the mother of Jesus, was absolutely the last thing on my mind. Having been raised as a Methodist, for me Mary had been primarily a figure who appeared in the Christmas story and then disappeared, with the exception of a few brief scriptural references. Ten years ago after a long spiritual search, I found what I had been looking for in the Eastern Orthodox Church. For Orthodox Christians, Mary has a central place of honor in our churches. We do not worship her, for that is reserved for God alone, but we do revere her and honor her as we believe Jesus would want us to do, as He did Himself. However, even though I have been an Orthodox Christian for nearly ten years, I must confess that I often didn't give Mary much thought except when I was in church.

That morning I began my day as I begin most days, sitting at my windowseat with a view of our backyard. I sit with my cup of coffee, my journal, the Bible, and often another spiritually uplifting book. I enjoy watching the squirrels and the birds. It's a peaceful way to begin my day, and I treasure that hour.

On that particular Thursday morning, the day before Good Friday, I was sitting quietly when the words "My name is Mary" came to my mind. I quickly wrote the words down in my journal along with a brief paragraph that is now the second paragraph of this book. Then I stopped because I had to work that day. During the day I thought about the words that I had written, and when I had time, I would find myself wondering what Mary's life must have been like. I think we often lose sight of the fact that she was a real woman with hopes and fears like all of us.

The next morning, Good Friday, I started writing, and the words flowed easily. Although I was aware of what I was writing, I didn't take time to edit what I was writing or to carefully choose my words. I wrote as quickly as the words would come to my mind. I wrote for three days, in between going to church several times and cooking Easter dinner. Finally during the evening of Easter Sunday, the words stopped coming. I still had another day off, and so I typed up the story I had written. Although in the weeks ahead I added more to the story, those first pages formed the essence of *My Name is Mary*, and most of those paragraphs have been left intact.

This was not what I had planned to do during my long weekend. Having four days off is a treat, and I had many things I hoped to get done during those days. Spending the time writing a book about Mary was not what I had planned for those days nor for the weeks ahead. The story began to take over my free time and my life.

At the beginning I wasn't sure why I was writing this, other than the fact that I felt that I had to do so. I thought that possibly it was simply for my own spiritual growth, and I was okay with that. However, when I began to share it with others, I came to realize that for whatever reason, I had been given a gift, and now it was my responsibility to share it.

This is not a book of theology. It is really a very simple story, the story of a mother and her child. If you are an Orthodox Christian or a Catholic, you have grown up with Mary being a presence in your faith. If you are a Protestant, perhaps giving much thought to Mary is new to you. It is not my intent or desire to attempt to convert anyone to my faith. There is beauty in all of the various ways Christians choose to worship our Lord. However, I do think that it is important to remember Mary. She carried Jesus in her womb. She was with Him as He grew from a child into an adult, nurturing both His body and His spirit. She was there for the first miracle. She was there when He died. She was there for the Resurrection. She was the most important person in His life, the last person He thought of when He was dying on the cross. I think it's important for us, 2000 years later, to remember her role in this amazing story.

– Denise Sawyer

My Name Is Mary

The Story of the Mother of Jesus

My Name is Mary

Nearly thirty years have passed since the miraculous events that have changed the world. I am old now, and I know that my life here among you will soon be over. As I sit here in my garden in the warm sunshine, I long to tell the story one more time, to one more person, and I pray that you will indulge me, even though you may have heard this story before.

My name is Mary. In the years to come, I fear that I will become almost a myth to some or perhaps to others of little importance in these events. I fear that people will forget that I was once a living and breathing person just like you. A child of God who was given an awesome responsibility and an incredible gift. My son's name is Jesus.

I was the only child of Anna and Joachim. I was a very loved child, a very wanted child. My parents had been married for many years without children. They prayed to our God, the God of Abraham, promising Him that if they were blessed with a child, they would dedicate their child, whether a son or a daughter, to the Temple. Their prayers were answered, and my mother found that although she was past the usual age of child-bearing, she had conceived a child, and I was born.

I have a few memories of the early years of my childhood. I remember my father's flocks, for he had many sheep. I remember our simple home and the smell of bread baking in the oven outside. I remember my mother's tender touch, and I know that I was very loved. I was also taught at an early age to love our God, for our faith was very much a part of our daily life.

When I was three years old, my parents fulfilled their vow to God, and they brought me to the Temple in Jerusalem, to the Court of Women. I did not understand why we were there. It seemed to be a special occasion, and I was dressed in new clothes; but my mother looked so sad. I remember walking the fifteen high steps up to the Court of Women, so many steps for such a small child. Once I reached the top, I was not afraid. Then I realized that my parents were leaving me there. My mother tried to explain, but I was so young, too young to understand. As they left the Court of Women, I tried not to cry. I wanted to be brave for them, but I remember crying and being comforted by the other girls and women in the Temple.

My parents often came to see me, although not as often as they would have liked, for they did not live in Jerusalem. My life settled into a routine and I was content, for it soon became the only life I really remembered, my brief early years living with my parents fading from my memory. I learned more about our God and our Scriptures, and I was taught about our prophecies. I learned to weave, becoming quite skilled. Then when I was about ten years old, I was told that my parents, who were quite elderly by that time, had died. I mourned their deaths and my loss. However, my cousin Elizabeth and her husband Zacharias occasionally visited me, and she became like a second mother to me. I looked forward to their visits.

———✑———

When it became clear that I was no longer a girl, but a maiden, the priests at the Temple, as well as Elizabeth and Zacharias, decided that I should no longer be living in the Court of Women. They wanted me to have a husband and a family. I would have been content to stay in the Temple living a life dedicated to God. However, I was told that one of the ways God is worshipped is by having children. They thought that I should have someone to protect me. I was reluctant to leave the security of my home in the Court of Women, where I had lived for over ten years, but I obeyed their wishes.

They found a husband for me, Joseph, who lived in Nazareth and had been a friend of my parents. He was much older than I and had been married for many years. His wife had died a year earlier after a long illness, leaving him with six children named James, Jude, Simon, Joses, Salome and Esther. James was the youngest, and he was still heartbroken over the loss of his mother. I was told that Joseph needed a wife to help take care of his young son James.

And so we were betrothed, which preceded our marriage by many months. Because I had nowhere else to live, having grown up in the Temple, I went to live in Joseph's house, along with several young friends from the Temple, to care for James. Then Joseph left for many months to build houses near the sea, for he was a carpenter by trade. I began an entirely new kind of life, living outside of the Temple for the first time in over ten years. I had much to learn, but Elizabeth came for a visit and helped me at the beginning.

One morning, several months after Joseph had left, I was at the well when I first heard the angel's words, but seeing no one, I was frightened, and I hurried back to Joseph's house. Then the angel appeared to me again. Angels, messengers from God, appeared to the prophets of old, but I was a mere girl, barely into womanhood, newly betrothed to Joseph. When I again heard the angel say, "Mary," I turned and looked around, not knowing who was calling me. The light was blinding, and I fell to my knees. Then the angel spoke strange words to me. He told me that I was blessed among women, that I would have a son and his name would be Jesus. I asked how that could be, for I had not known a man. The angel said that the Holy Spirit would come upon me, that my son would be the Son of God.

Although I felt myself to be unworthy of such an honor, I had no doubt that what the angel said to me was true. The world that God has created is filled with wonders and miracles. How could I doubt that I would become part of another miracle, that I would give birth to a child without ever having known a man. I didn't understand, but I knew it would be true. I felt humbled by the gift. I knew that my life would never be the same nor would it turn out the way I had expected, but it never occurred to me to say "No." There was no choice. This was my destiny. A cloud of mist surrounded me, and as it faded I found myself alone.

Once that strange day had passed, I sometimes wondered if perhaps I had imagined the whole thing. But then within several months I could see subtle changes in my body, and I knew that what the angel had told me was true. Although I was not really frightened by what was happening, for I trusted in God, I had many questions, and I needed time to try to begin to understand what was happening to me before Joseph returned home. I wanted to talk to Elizabeth. I had always felt close to her, especially during the years after my parents' deaths. There was a connection between us. There was even more of a connection than I realized at the time. Our lives would be intertwined in ways I did not then understand.

I took James to stay with his sister Salome, who had recently married a fisherman named Zebedee, and I, accompanied by my friends from the Temple, went to Ein Karem where Elizabeth and Zacharias lived, a journey of about five days. There were always many travelers on the road, and so we never really felt frightened, traveling in the company of other women. I felt that God would be watching over me, protecting the new life within me. The journey there gave me time to think about what had happened and time to find peace with it.

Elizabeth and her husband Zacharias had never had children, although that had always been her fondest wish. Now, after so many years, she was finally with child. Shortly before, her husband, a priest in the temple, had mysteriously become mute. It was a difficult time for Elizabeth as her pregnancy advanced. I was happy to have a good excuse to visit with her.

However, before I even had a chance to tell her my news, she knew. The baby in her womb moved suddenly when I came into her presence, and she spoke the same words as the angel, that I was blessed among women. While I was with Elizabeth, I had time to ponder all that the angel had said. He had told me that my son was to be named Jesus and that he would save his people from their sins. Was my son to be the long-awaited Messiah? I was puzzled by the meaning of it all, including why I had been chosen by God for this honor. Why me when so many were more worthy? Elizabeth was like a second mother to me, and I shared with her much of what the angel had told me, although not everything. Some words I kept hidden in my heart.

I stayed with her for several months, helping her through the final months of her pregnancy, easing the burden of her daily chores. We talked long hours about the sons that we would bear. I stayed with her until after the birth of her son. Her husband miraculously regained his voice after his son's birth, and he announced that the child's name was John. Then I knew it was time to return to my home in Nazareth, before traveling became too difficult for me.

———

Earlier I had begun to feel the first faint fluttering within, like butterfly wings, and I knew that my son was healthy and growing within me. By the time I returned to Nazareth, my condition was becoming more difficult to conceal. Joseph was confused and angry when he returned. He had left me a virgin, and he returned to find me with child. He demanded to know who had done this to me. I wept, trying to explain to him that I had not known a man. However, I could understand his confusion and his anger. I was frightened by what he might do. He had every right, according to our Law, to send me away, to have me condemned, to have me stoned, for I had conceived a child outside of marriage. Once again I prayed to God that He watch over me and the child growing within me. God heard my weeping and answered my prayers, for an angel appeared to Joseph also, putting his fears to rest. He did not fully understand, but he knew that I had not been unfaithful to him and accepted me as his wife.

I had lived in Joseph's house for many months with James and my friends from the temple. It seemed strange at first to have just the three of us there, Joseph, James and myself. Joseph and I were content together, although both of us lived much within ourselves at that time. All of this was still so very new, so very mysterious. Sometimes we did not have the words to express what we were thinking, what we felt. At the time, I suppose, I felt mostly gratitude to him that he had not sent me away in shame when he learned of my condition, which would have been his right. But then gratitude turned into contentment and contentment into love, especially after Jesus was born and I saw that Joseph loved him and would be a true father to him.

As I grew larger with child, everyone assumed that Joseph was the father. I would have been risking my life and the life of the child if I had tried to tell people the truth. Joseph would be my son's father in every other way, loving this child and teaching him the ways of God.

The last few months passed quickly, and Joseph and I would sometimes talk quietly of the mystery that had taken over our lives. When I felt the new life moving within me, I would feel such joy, such contentment, and such an awesome sense of responsibility.

———

As the time of the birth grew closer, we were distressed to learn that the Roman Emperor Caesar Augustus had ordered everyone in Palestine to return to the place of their ancestors to be counted for a census for taxation purposes. We would have to make the five-day journey to Bethlehem, home of Joseph's kinsmen. I was frightened, for I had hoped to have my baby at home in Nazareth. Joseph tried to find some way to delay the trip or at least get permission for me to stay behind while he was gone. However, the officials were not sympathetic to our needs, and so I was required to go with him.

Joseph borrowed a donkey for me to ride on since he knew that I could not walk the entire way to Bethlehem. We packed up a few provisions into a straw bag, filled the goatskin bag with water, and we were on our way. We traveled with Joseph's sons and their families, who were also required to make the journey to Bethlehem.

Because of the emperor's decree, there were many travelers on the road. As was our custom, the men and women usually traveled separately. However, Joseph was very protective of me, and during the day we often traveled together. Young James usually chose to walk with us at those times, leading my donkey as we journeyed to Bethlehem, for he and I had formed a close bond during the months when Joseph was gone. At night I would stay with the other women, and they were a comfort to me, often giving me extra bedding to rest upon or a bit of extra food. I felt that God was continuing to watch over me and the child.

It was a long journey for a woman so far along with child. I was often lost in thought. When we stopped at a well a half-day's journey from Bethlehem, Joseph commented that sometimes I seemed happy and sometimes sad. I confessed to him that although I was often filled with joy about the miracle within me, I was also frightened for my unborn son. I knew that many would rejoice at his birth, for we had long been promised a Messiah. However, I feared that many would refuse to accept him. I was also frightened about giving birth so far away from our home in Nazareth. Joseph reminded me of the prophecies about the Messiah, that he would be born in Bethlehem, and once again my fears vanished, and I felt at peace, knowing that all was in the hands of God.

As we approached Bethlehem, the pains were beginning, and I knew that my time was near. We began to look for a place to stay, first among Joseph's kinsmen who lived there; but because so many people had returned to the town, it was very crowded. When we came to the last place, the innkeeper and his wife had pity on me, seeing my condition. They gave us shelter in a stable, which had been carved out of the hillside where they kept their animals. It was not where I had expected to give birth to my child, but it was cozy and warm. The innkeeper gave us fresh sweet-smelling hay for me to lie on, and his wife sent for a midwife to help in the delivery of my child.

It was not a difficult birth, for the Lord eased the way into the world for His son, and he arrived shortly before the arrival of Zelomi, the midwife. Zelomi, along with a kinswoman, Salome, washed my newborn son, rubbing his small body with salt, water, and oil. Then they wrapped him in swaddling cloths, and soon I was holding my newborn child in my arms, taking him to my breast. I was filled with such love. I also felt fear, for

I knew that this was no ordinary child. This child was holy. His life would take him places I could not then imagine. However, I tried not to worry about what was to come, and I thanked God for the safe delivery of my son.

We had visitors later that night, in the early morning hours. Shepherds from the nearby fields came to the stable. They said that they had seen a very bright star shining over the stable and that an angel had appeared to them. They went and told others, but few believed them, for we were left mostly in peace. Even the animals in the stable seemed to sense that something out of the ordinary had happened, for they were quietly watching us, not disturbed by our presence.

—⁊⁊⁊—

On the eighth day after his birth, Joseph took our son to be circumcised, in the tradition of the God of Abraham and Jacob. He announced that the child's name was Jesus. Afterwards, I comforted our son at my breast.

During the forty days of my purification after having given birth, we stayed in Bethlehem. Joseph found a room for us in the home of Salome. It was while we were staying in her home that three strange men arrived. They were very finely dressed and brought gifts to give to Jesus: gold, myrrh, and frankincense. They told us that they had come from the East, having also followed a sign in the heavens. We could not understand all that they said, but I knew that they also had a role to play in these events. Then they left and we never heard from them again.

After the forty days, we were preparing to return to Nazareth. We first went to Jerusalem, which was near Bethlehem. It is a tradition of our faith to present the first-born son at the Temple, and we took Jesus there. Joseph offered a sacrifice of two turtledoves, which was all that we could afford.

Despite all that I knew concerning his mysterious conception, I felt an ordinary mother's love for my child. I knew deep down in my soul that he was a very special child, that he was the son of our God. However,

because he was still just a helpless babe in my arms, not yet aware of his true nature, it was somewhat of a surprise to me that others were aware of his holiness. Simeon at the temple reached out to hold him, immediately sensing who he was, praising and thanking God for the privilege of having seen the child. Holding Jesus in his arms, he prophesied about him, which filled me with fear for the future. Anna, an elderly prophetess at the temple, also recognized him and told others of him. Perhaps they thought her crazy, for no one pursued us.

—⟡—

The king, Herod, must have heard of the search by the three strange men, for he wanted to know where the child was that they had sought. When they left without revealing the truth to him, he became angry and ordered the death of all the young male children under the age of two years living in Bethlehem and in the surrounding area, hoping to kill the young king who was rumored to

be among them. Joseph was once again visited by an angel in a dream, and he was warned of the danger. We fled to Egypt, where we lived until we were told by the angel that the king was dead and it was safe to return to the land of our people. I later learned that Elizabeth had escaped with her son John into the mountains, seeking refuge in a cave. Zacharias had been killed by soldiers at the temple when he refused to tell them where his young son had been taken.

The journey to Egypt took many weeks. Because we had very little money for such a lengthy journey, we used some of the gold that the three strangers had given to Jesus to pay for food and lodging as we traveled to safety in Egypt. When we finally arrived, it was our home for over three years.

During our years in exile, we tried to live as normal a life as possible, even though we were strangers in a foreign land. Joseph found occasional carpentry jobs to help provide for our small family, and we often rented a room or two in the home of other Jews living in Egypt. Occasionally he would find us a small house.

However, we did not stay in one place. We continued to fear the long arm of King Herod, even in Egypt. Even though there was nothing unusual or special about Jesus' appearance, for he was just a baby, there would be times when others would be perceptive enough to realize that he was not an ordinary child, just as Simeon and Anna had at the Temple in Jerusalem, and they would begin to ask questions. When that would happen, we would quietly pack up our meager belongings, say goodbye to the few friends we might have made there, and move on. This happened frequently enough that we never really put down roots in any one spot. And yet it was not just fear that made us move on, made us restless. We missed our homeland, and we were looking forward to eventually returning to our families.

The years of exile were not without their own pleasures, for we had our son and we had James with us. Jesus was such a delight as a baby, only crying briefly when hungry, although not for long for I quickly took him to my breast. He was very easy to care for during

our years in Egypt. He was so healthy. I don't remember him ever having been sick. James was such a good big brother to Jesus. He was fascinated by him and very protective of him. As Jesus grew older, James would sometimes carry him for me, introducing him to the world around him. As he began to walk and to explore that world, James would be there to make sure that he would be safe. Life was good during our years of exile. We had shelter, food on our table, and we had our sons. Our needs were simple and we were content.

———

Eventually Joseph was told by the angel that King Herod was dead and that it was safe to return home. It was so wonderful to be back in the land of our fathers. We rejoiced to see Nazareth in the distance, nestled at the side of a mountain. We were home again, surrounded by Joseph's other children and our kinsmen and friends. Life began to settle into a comfortable routine that would continue for many years to come. I

was content with taking care of my home, my garden, and my family. Joseph went back to his work as a carpenter, building houses and furniture for families in Nazareth. James became an apprentice to Joseph, learning the trade of his father just as his older brothers had done before him.

After the mysterious events surrounding Jesus' conception, Joseph and I were faithful companions, affectionate to each other, kind to each other. However, we never became intimate in the way of husband and wife. Our intimacy was in the shared responsibility of raising this very special child. My womb remained closed after the birth of Jesus.

While Jesus was still very young, he tended to stay close to me as I worked at home and in the garden. He would go with me on my daily trips to the market and to the well. He had a child's natural curiosity about the small creatures that also inhabit this world of ours. As a child, he always cared for the small wounded animals that he would find. He would often bring home tiny birds with broken wings and other small creatures for me to tend. Once a tiny bird flew from his suddenly opened hand. I had thought the bird to be dead, but perhaps I was mistaken. Or possibly this was an early sign of his power to heal. I don't know.

His fascination with everything in this world continued, and as he grew older, he began to ask more and more questions. As soon as he could begin to understand, I began to teach him of our God and our faith. I taught him the verses of Scripture that are the foundation of our faith. "Hear O Israel: The Lord our God is one Lord. And thou shalt love the Lord thy God with all thy mind, and with all thy soul, and with all thy strength." We had daily prayers and went to the synagogue on the Sabbath to hear the Scripture read by one of the men in the community.

—◦◦◦—

When Jesus was six years old, he began to attend daily classes at the synagogue, where the Jewish boys of Nazareth received the only formal education available to them. No such education was available for the girls, for most of what they were expected to know as wives and mothers could be learned at home. Having spent most of my childhood in the Temple in Jerusalem, I was an exception.

The rabbis would read from the scrolls, and the boys would first learn to memorize and later to read parts of Scripture. They would use hard pieces of cane to practice writing on pieces of broken pottery, with wax on a wooden tablet, or more frequently, in the dirt. Jesus was so proud the day he first came home and wrote a short verse in the dirt outside our home.

When he was about ten, he was able to join the class of older boys. They would be allowed to begin discussing questions of the Law with their teachers. Sometimes Jesus would come home eager to talk about what he had learned; other times he seemed to need to be alone to contemplate what the teachers had taught. His mind was always open; he was always learning, always questioning. Sometimes his questions went beyond our understanding, and we were grateful to be able to send him to his teachers at the synagogue with his questions. Even then, as a boy, he was not always satisfied with their answers, although out of respect for them, he did not argue or disagree with them.

—∽∾∽—

Every year at Passover, we would go to the Temple in Jerusalem. Women were not required to make such a journey every year, for we often have too many responsibilites with home and family, but it was important to me to make this yearly journey to Jerusalem. This was a special occasion to honor our God and a pleasant break from the usual routine. We always traveled with many family and friends, men and women traveling in separate groups, as was our custom. Children could travel with either parent.

On our way home to Nazareth the year that Jesus was twelve years old, we suddenly realized that he was not with us. I had not seen him since we had started our journey back to Nazareth. I had assumed that he was traveling with Joseph and the other men; Joseph thought that he was with me. When we realized that he was with neither of us and that no one had seen him, we hurried back to Jerusalem, fearing for the safety of our young son, alone in a large city. We found him at the temple, surrounded by elders. He was asking questions, learning as much as possible from them, and teaching them just as they were teaching him. He seemed surprised to see us, for he had not realized that we were gone. He said that we should have known that he would be in his Father's house. Then he hugged me and told me that he had not meant to worry us, and he promised not to do that again.

—⁓—

I suppose that he was not really a beautiful child, although to a mother's eyes her children are always beautiful. There was nothing about him that would make people stop and stare at his beauty. However, he had a presence about him that made people aware of him and listen to him. And he was so very kind. He actually resembled his earthly father, Joseph, although they were not of the same blood. They shared the same dark and slightly curly hair, the dark brooding eyes, the gentle smile, and strong hands. No one ever suspected that Joseph was not his blood father.

Joseph was his father in every other way. He cared for him, loved him, taught him the faith of his fathers, and he taught him the trade that Jesus practiced until he was thirty years old. At the end of the day, they would often go on long walks together into the hills around Nazareth. They would talk, but I think that Joseph often learned more from Jesus than the other way around.

Because Joseph had children from his first wife, Jesus grew up with many kinsmen around him. Salome, Joseph's youngest daughter, had married a fisherman named Zebedee, with whom she had two sons, James and John, both younger than Jesus. Joseph's other children also had married and had children, and so Jesus had no lack of companions as he grew up. He enjoyed playing the usual childhood games, although there were times when he chose to be alone.

Occasionally Elizabeth would come for a visit with her son John. He was a very serious and solitary child, content to spend long hours alone. Jesus always looked forward to their visits. He and John would wander off by themselves for hours. We tried not to worry about them when they would be late getting home, for we knew that they would be deep in conversation, not aware of the passage of time. I think Jesus looked forward to his visits because with John he could talk about more serious matters than he could with his other friends.

Elizabeth died before John was fully grown into manhood. We asked him to come and live with us, but he seemed content to be alone. His needs were few, and he was very mature for his young years. We did not hear too much about him for a while, other than that he was alive and well; but in the years ahead, we began to hear of his preaching.

—◦◦◦—

I think that acceptance of who Jesus truly was came gradually to us. Although Joseph and I often talked quietly about the mysterious events surrounding his birth and about his unusual interests and compassion for all living creatures, we tried not to treat him as if he were anything other than a normal child. It seemed important that we give him a firm foundation for whatever future lay ahead of him.

We also talked about our fears for him and his future. We both knew the prophecies about the long-awaited Messiah. We knew that the people were expecting someone different from what Jesus would be. They wanted an earthly king who would free our people from the oppression of the Romans. Jesus did not seem to be growing up to be that kind of a leader.

As he grew older, he began to realize that he was different from the other boys, although I don't think he understood why. When I sensed that he was ready, I began to gradually share with him the story of his miraculous conception and his birth, as well as the importance of keeping the information to himself. I think it took him a while to fully understand what I was telling him. Once he did, he accepted it as something that perhaps he had known all along, deep within his soul. It explained why he had always felt so different from other boys. It did not change his relationship with Joseph, for which I was grateful.

———

And so Jesus grew up, gradually becoming a man. He was well-liked, this son of Joseph and Mary, the carpenter's son. He began to work with Joseph in his carpenter's shop. There would also be times when he would go off into the hills to be alone for several days at a time, sometimes weeks. We tried not to worry; we knew that he had much to think about, much to sort out in his mind. He needed time alone to think about just what it was that God wanted him to do with his life.

As Jesus grew into manhood, Joseph seemed to age more quickly. He was many years older than I, and the years began to catch up with him. After one particularly bad attack, Joseph took to his bed. Jesus and I were there at his bedside, taking care of him, comforting him, and in the end, letting him go. Several of Joseph's children were there as well. Jude and Simon, as well as James, had settled in Nazareth, also following the trade that their father had taught them. Salome lived nearby with her husband Zebedee and their sons James and John. Only God knows how much time is allotted to each life. Joseph's life was over, and so I had to tell my faithful husband and companion good-bye.

In the years that followed Jesus took over the carpenter shop, providing for me. He was a good son and a good friend. We began to talk even more about his birth, our God, what it all meant. I think that we both knew that being a carpenter was not what he was supposed to be doing with his life forever, but he felt a loyalty to me not to leave me alone and an obligation to take care of me since Joseph was gone. However, we knew that eventually the time would come for him to begin the true path and purpose of his life.

Jesus would have been a wonderful husband and

father, and at one point in his life, I wished for him that kind of life. It would have been so much easier than what God had planned for him. After Joseph died, Jesus and I discussed it. Although he hadn't yet felt that the time was right for him to begin his true work, he knew that the time would come, and that when it did, it would be unfair to burden a wife and children with the kind of life he would lead.

—◦◦◦—

When Jesus was thirty, he somehow knew deep within himself that the time was approaching. He went to John, now known as John the Baptist, to be baptised by him. He and John had had many serious discussions about God when they were younger. John must have sensed something holy about Jesus, for he was reluctant to baptise him, saying that he should be baptised by Jesus instead, but Jesus insisted. As he came up out of the water, some of those who were there said that a dove appeared out of the heavens and landed on Jesus and that a voice was heard saying, "This is my beloved Son." But others heard and saw nothing and did not believe.

For Jesus, this was the beginning. He heard the voice, he felt the Holy Spirit becoming one with him. He suddenly knew without a doubt just who he was. Knowing your destiny can be overwhelming, so after a brief farewell to me so that I would not worry, he went off into the hills for forty days and forty nights, refusing the food and water I wanted him to take with him. I think that this was a test he felt he must go through. When he came back, he was thinner, but stronger as well, and he seemed to have a new sureness about him. However, he didn't immediately begin to preach, seeming reluctant to begin what he undoubtedly knew would be a difficult mission.

By the time Jesus began his ministry, he was no longer a young man. He was thirty years old, of an age when men often have several children. His hair already had a few strands of gray, although many more would appear during the three years ahead, and the lines in his face had deepened after his ordeal in the desert. Perhaps

God in His wisdom knew that the words of a mature man would have more impact than those of a very young man.

After his forty days in the desert, he began gathering his disciples, good and decent men from all walks of life. These were men who literally dropped everything to follow him and learn from him. James and John, the sons of Zebedee and kinsmen, were among the first. They had been followers of John the Baptist, and they had been at the Jordan River the day that Jesus had been baptised. They were among those who had heard the voice of God and had seen the dove. After John the Baptist had been arrested, they came to our home, looking for Jesus. I told them that he had gone into the wilderness to be alone. They returned to Capernaum, where they were fishermen, working for Simon Peter and Andrew, two brothers. When Jesus returned, he sought them out. The four of them immediately went with Jesus, following their hearts and changing their lives forever. During the weeks and months ahead, he continued to gather his disciples, twelve in all.

One day shortly after Jesus had begun gathering his disciples, we were invited to a wedding feast in Cana. It was the wedding of good friends from the village, and the feast had been going on for several days. The guests were enjoying themselves. However, I began to notice worried expressions on the faces of the father of the bride and the bridegroom. They were concerned that they were running out of wine. I knew that it would be very embarrassing for them not to have enough wine for the guests, and so I decided to intercede.

I knew that Jesus had the power to create new wine for them, for I had seen him quietly perform small miracles before. He was reluctant, saying that it was not yet the time to reveal himself, but at my insistence, he obeyed. And so it began. I didn't understand his reluctance to perform this first miracle. I think that perhaps he held back, knowing that once he took that first simple step and performed his first public miracle, his ministry would truly begin and there would be no turning back. He knew that his life would never be the same. Perhaps it's like walking into a heavy fog or mist, not being able to see just where the next step will take you. And possibly he knew from the very beginning where this would all lead, which would explain his hesitation at taking that first step.

———✦———

After Jesus started his ministry, teaching in the synagogues as well as out among the people, he and his newly gathered group of disciples made their base in Capernaum, on the shores of the Sea of Galilee, often staying at Peter's home. Peter's mother-in-law, who became a good friend of mine, was always very happy to see them. She would feed them and find pallets for them to sleep on. In the evenings she would sit quietly in the corner and listen as Jesus and his disciples talked, and so her own conversion began.

Wherever he went, people would surround him, to touch him, to hear his words. Some would come hoping for a miracle, to be cured of some affliction. He would touch the eyes of the blind and they would see. He would touch the crippled limbs of the lame and they would walk. He would touch the faces of the lepers and they would be made clean. One woman was healed of a long affliction by merely touching the hem of his garment.

It bothered him a bit, I think, that so many followed him for the miracles rather than for the teaching. However, many stayed to listen to him, to learn from him. He spoke simply to the people, often in parables. He taught them as much as they had the ability to understand. He spoke with such authority and with such love and compassion. Alone with his disciples, his teaching would go into greater depth, stretching the limits of their understanding. Much of what he taught them only made sense later, after he was gone.

He taught about a God who seemed different from the God of our fathers, who often appeared to be a vengeful and frightening God. This God that Jesus spoke of was a loving God, but also a powerful God, to be respected. Some people accused Jesus of following a different God, but the God of our fathers and the God of Jesus were the same. Jesus was sent to enlighten us, to give us a fuller understanding of our God.

———*œœ*———

I remained at home at the beginning of his ministry. I often heard reports of the healings, his teachings, of the large crowds that followed him. I was grateful that he had finally answered the call of his Father, but I also missed him terribly. His presence in our home had created an energy, and his absence now created a void. I was worried for him, as any mother would be. I was concerned that he was not eating well, that he often had no comfortable place to sleep. And I worried for his physical safety, for large crowds can become unruly.

When he started his ministry, some of his kinsmen were as skeptical as the priests in the temple who felt threatened by his teachings. I myself had become increasingly fearful for his safety because of the crowds, as was James, who had always been very protective of Jesus. One day Joseph's sons and I went to see Jesus, to speak privately with him, but he would not see us at that time. I realized then that I could not let our all-too-human fears keep him from doing the will of his Father. Once that moment of weakness passed, we became more accepting of the danger, more accepting of God's will. Despite their initial reservations, several of his brothers actually became devout followers and became active in the church after the Resurrection.

As Jesus began to spend more time traveling all over the countryside, our times alone together became less frequent. There were so many demands on him, and I think he knew that he only had a short time to accomplish what God had sent him to do. Because our time together was limited, those moments became all the more precious. If he were near Nazareth with his disciples, he would sometimes come and spend the night, and we would have a chance to talk.

—◦◦◦—

Men were the first to hear Jesus speak and became the first followers. As his ministry grew, more and more women were drawn to his words. Jesus knew that the things he had been sent to teach were meant for the ears of all people, men and women. From the beginning, he had a different attitude toward women than was the custom. Men did not traditionally speak to women in public, but Jesus talked as freely to the women as he did to the men. He welcomed them to listen to him, even to follow him if that was what their hearts told them to do. Women, by the nature of our lives as wives and mothers, are bound by the responsibilities of home. I did not travel with Jesus and his disciples at the beginning, for women did not traditionally travel with men. However, as his ministry grew, women in a position to be able to travel with him chose to do so, and Jesus welcomed them.

Often it was the widows who were most free to follow their hearts. Salome, Joseph's youngest daughter, had been recently widowed. When Jesus and his disciples were near Nazareth, she would often accompany me, along with several other women, to hear him speak and to see her sons James and John. She, like her sons, began to believe. The circle of women who traveled with Jesus grew larger. Mary, wife of Cleopas, a brother of Joseph, had also been widowed, and Jesus' message struck a chord deep within, and she believed. I think that perhaps the women who had known him from the past were often more receptive to his words then the men were, who had difficulty reconciling such words of wisdom coming from someone they had known for years.

As time went on, I began to travel more frequently with Jesus and his disciples. The other women and I usually stayed slightly apart from the disciples and other men. I became friends with many of the women I met through Jesus. I would usually stay in the background. I was content, along with some of the other women, to prepare meals for the disciples and my son. It was important to me that I be a part of all of this, as much as possible, for I felt that I had had a role in this story from the very beginning.

Often when I was standing there at the edge of the crowd, I would feel Jesus' eyes upon me. He would smile, and I would feel the connection between us. Sometimes he would seek me out in the early evening hours, and we would walk and talk contentedly together, just as he had earlier done with Joseph on their evening walks in the hills around Nazareth. At these moments, he would sometimes confide his fears to me. Despite his fears, he had learned to trust in God's wisdom.

Women would often bring their children with them to hear Jesus speak, and the children would gather around him. They wanted to touch him and to be touched by him. This bothered the disciples, especially at the beginning; but Jesus would gently chastise them, for he loved the children and welcomed them into his arms. He knew that his message was not only for the men and women, but for the children as well, who sometimes have the ears to hear and understand what their elders do not.

—⟶

Even though I had read the Scriptures and knew of the prophecies about the Messiah, I think that complete understanding of his divinity came to me slowly. I had known from the beginning that Jesus was a very special and unique gift from God; however, he was also my son. I had carried him in my womb and then in my arms. I had nursed him at my breast and watched him grow from a child into an adult. I knew that he had a powerful message for the world, but it was not until later, after the Resurrection, that I truly understood that he was both my son and my God. I cannot explain it, for it is a mystery; but the knowledge fills me with joy.

Jesus was such a forgiving man, and he tried to teach us the importance of forgiveness, for bitterness can destroy the soul. He could see deep down inside a person to see who he really was. That was how he was with Mary Magdalene, who also became my good friend. She had struggled with many demons for years, and she had been mocked and scorned. Jesus understood that sometimes the circumstances of our lives can distort and hide who we really are. He could tell that in her soul, she was good and pure. When he forgave her, accepted her, and loved her, she was able to forgive herself. She became a totally different person, a loving and vital part of our small community both before and after Jesus' death. And Jesus loved her, giving her the blessing of being one of the very first to see his resurrected body. Those precious moments alone with her risen Lord sustained her in the years ahead. She never went back to the life she had lived before Jesus had come into her life.

I think that one of the most important things that Jesus tried to teach us is that we should love. We should love our God, we should love our neighbor, and we should love ourselves, for both we and our neighbors are children of God. How can we not love what God has created?

As with any group of people spending so much time together, there were sometimes conflicts among the disciples. On one such occasion Salome, the mother of James and John, caused a brief period of tension when she misunderstood Jesus' message about the Kingdom

49

of Heaven. She confused the heavenly Kingdom with an earthly one when she asked Jesus to give her two sons seats of honor, thrones on each side of Jesus. He chastised her for making such a request, but he also forgave her for her misunderstanding of his teaching.

Despite the seriousness of his message, Jesus loved God's gift of life. Although he had few material needs, he loved the world around him. He enjoyed being with his friends, both his disciples and old friends such as Lazarus and his sisters Martha and Mary, as well as many new friends. He enjoyed attending their wedding feasts, celebrating with them the good things in their lives. On such occasions, he could be in a playful mood, laughing with his disciples, gently teasing them. He knew that they needed time to relax, time to think about less serious matters. However, just as he could laugh with his friends, he could also mourn with them. When he and his disciples received word that his cousin John had been killed in prison, he wept with them, and then he went off by himself for a while to mourn and to pray.

As time went by, he found it increasingly difficult to be alone, for the crowds always found him. There were always so many who were in need of his healing touch or who were hungry for his healing words, and he gave of himself freely to them.

———∞———

There are many among us and in nearby lands who do not worship the God of Abraham. They often prefer to worship many smaller but less powerful gods. That somehow seems easier for them to understand than one all-powerful God. I believe that God is a mystery, beyond our limited understanding.

The disciples were shocked one day to find Jesus talking to a Samaritan woman at a well in the city of Sychar. While they had gone to buy food, Jesus had met the woman at the well and started talking to her. During their conversation he told her many things about herself, and she came to believe that he might be the Christ. She went into town and told many people about this man she had met at the well, and the people sought him out and asked him to stay and teach them. Jesus and his disciples stayed there for two days. The disciples had not expected this, for they thought that the teachings of Jesus were for the Jewish people alone.

Years later, after the Resurrection, this same Samaritan woman went to Jerusalem to be baptised by Peter. She was given the name of Photini, and when I last heard of her, she and her sons and daughters were in Carthage, teaching others about Jesus.

—◦◦◦—

I got to know the disciples well, some better than others. They were all so very different. The one thing they had in common was that they loved my son and gave up their old lives to follow him and learn from him. James and John, of course, I had known since they were babies. John has always been one of my favorites. I think he was one of Jesus' favorites as well, although he tried not to show partiality. Peter was a natural leader among the disciples. He was a large man, easily standing out in a crowd, but he was also very gentle. Judas Iscariot seemed a bit aloof, often too preoccupied with the things of this world. I did not feel as close to him as to some of the others. However, despite his later betrayal, I think that in his own way, he loved Jesus, but it became distorted and he lost sight of just who Jesus really was.

The three years seemed to pass quickly, and the years were filled with such wonders. So many people were drawn to his teachings, and the crowds continued to grow. As the years passed, I became increasingly concerned. His words were like drinks of fresh sweet water to the people, but the elders of the temple felt threatened by him, as did the civil authorities. The elders felt that he was teaching an entirely new religion. He was really teaching a fulfillment of the old, but they could not or would not understand.

Many of the earlier followers had turned away. They were expecting a Messiah who would crush the oppressors of our people. When they saw that Jesus was not the kind of Messiah they were expecting, they turned their backs on him and returned to their homes and their lives, continuing to wait for their earthly king.

When Jesus rode into Jerusalem on a donkey that final Passover, the crowds were so happy to see him, waving palm branches and laying them on the ground in his path. They seemed to have so much love for him, or so it seemed at the time. In a matter of days the crowds had turned on him, calling for his death. At the time I could not understand how things had changed so quickly. Looking back, I now realize that everything happened according to God's will. There was a time and a purpose for everything.

———⟨∾∾⟩———

When I heard that he had been arrested in the Garden of Gethsemene, betrayed by one of his own, my heart broke. I tried to find out what was happening to him, where he was; but his disciples had all scattered, too cowardly to remain with him. Some denied even having known him. I finally found John, who told me as much as he knew. I learned that Jesus had been passed back and forth between two evil men, betrayed by the crowds who had followed him.

Then I learned that he was to be crucified as if he were a common criminal. We hurried through the main streets in Jerusalem hoping for a glimpse of him. When we finally saw him, he was beaten and bloody, half-naked and carrying a large wooden cross. He looked so sorrowful, so defeated. John and I, as well as Mary Magdalene and the other women, hurried to Golgatha, where the crucifixion took place. We watched in horror as they pounded the nails into his hands and feet. We were not allowed close at the beginning, but eventually we eased our way nearer to the cross. The crowds were mocking him, these same crowds who had seen miracles performed by him. Soldiers were gambling for his cloak. They were making sport of him, and my heart was breaking. Earlier he had tried to prepare me for what was to come, but nothing can prepare a mother to see her only son tortured and killed.

Our God was merciful and He did not let His son suffer for days as was common in the slow death by crucifixion. By mid-afternoon it was obvious that the end was near. As I stood nearby, Jesus looked at John, his loyal disciple, and asked him to take care of me, to become my son. Although he was near death, one of his last thoughts was of me, of concern for me. He spoke his last words, surrendered his soul to God, and then he went limp. It was over. A terrible storm broke out, and people began running away in fear. However, John and I and the women stayed closeby, weeping for our loss, for the world's loss. Finally the soldiers took him down from the cross, and I cradled his broken body in my arms and I wept. I did not understand that this was just the beginning.

We were poor Galileans, far from our own towns and villages, with little money and no place to bury Jesus. Joseph of Arimathea, a wealthy follower who was also a member of the Council, offered his own unused tomb. He went to Pilate and begged permission from him to put the body in his tomb. The body of my son was carried there, wrapped in a white cloth and covered with spices, and placed on a wooden stretcher. Because the next day was the Sabbath, we were not able to return until the third day after his death.

—*∞*—

The Sabbath was such a sorrowful day. All of the disciples, including the women who had loved him, were inconsolable. It was a time of great confusion and pain. Part of the disciples' pain was because they had not been with Jesus during his ordeal. Most of them had fled after he had been arrested, afraid for their own lives. Peter denied three times having even known him. He confided his deep shame and regret to me, telling me that Jesus had foretold what Peter would do. They knew later that Jesus had forgiven them for their human weaknesses, and that he loved them.

The disciples slowly found their way to each other to comfort each other, to try and understand what had happened, why it had all gone so terribly wrong. There was anger and there were accusations, but mostly there was sorrow and a feeling of loss. They sensed that somehow they were to continue with Jesus' ministry, but they had no idea how to begin. Their hearts were not in it.

The next day the miraculous happened. The women disciples and I had made arrangements to rise early and be at the tomb at dawn. Mary Magdalene had been staying with me and, because we had had difficulty sleeping, we arose very early and went to the tomb to put more spices on my son's body. A large stone had been put at the entrance to the cave. When we got there, we immediately saw that the stone had been moved. There was a young man in front of the tomb, and he told us that Jesus was not there. We were told that he was gone. We did not understand. The young man said nothing else, but when I looked at him again, I thought that perhaps he was an angel. He looked familiar to me, as if he were someone I had seen many years earlier. However, I was confused and frightened, so I was not sure if I was thinking clearly. Mary Magdalene went hurrying off to find the disciples, to tell them that Jesus' body was missing.

While I was alone at the tomb, Jesus appeared to me. My eyes recognized Him immediately. He only spoke a few words to me, but He touched my hand, and I felt the warmth of His body. The memories of thirty-three years flooded through me. I knew that God had given me another miracle, and I knew that my Son would be part of me forever. None of our lives would ever be the same.

A short time later Salome and Joanna arrived, along with Mary, wife of Cleopas, Susanna, and Martha and Mary. They too saw that Jesus' body was missing, and they ran to find the disciples before I had a chance to talk to them, to tell them that I had seen Him with my own eyes.

Mary Magdalene had hurried to tell Peter and John that someone had taken their Lord's body out of the tomb, and as soon as they heard her words, they ran ahead of her to the tomb. They found the grave clothes just as they had left them in the tomb, as if still wrapped around a body, but the body was not there. Puzzled, they returned to the other disciples.

Then Mary Magdalene returned to the tomb, and as she stood there weeping, Jesus suddenly appeared to her and called her name. She dropped to her knees when she saw Him, so overwhelmed with joy that she was trembling. Afterwards, she hurried to tell the disciples that she had seen the risen Lord, but they did not believe.

He then appeared to the other women who were returning from the tomb. They also told the men what they had seen and heard, and still they did not believe what they considered idle tales from women.

Later, Jesus appeared to the disciples. He chastised them for their unbelief, and once again, He forgave them. I have sometimes wondered why it was that He appeared first to the women who loved Him, for the disciples also loved Him. However, women have a strength that comes from within, that is not related to physical strength. We were there when He was crucified; we were there when He suffered and died. We did not hide or flee out of fear for our own lives, and He blessed us by appearing to us first.

———

When He began to appear to those who had loved Him, it was a joyful time, beyond all understanding. How could this be possible? We had seen Him die with our own eyes, we had seen Joseph take His body to the tomb. It was a miracle. Perhaps it was easier for me to understand and accept, for I had been part of this miraculous story from the beginning.

He appeared to all of His disciples and closest followers over the next forty days, although He was not with us continuously. He would appear in the midst of us, and then just as suddenly, He would be gone. When He was with us, He continued to teach His disciples, preparing them for what was to come. He taught them the Mysteries of the Church. He had not revealed all of these to them before because they would not have understood. They did not truly realize who He was. They were not ready. Now they were, and their minds and their hearts were like empty vessels being filled with the purest of wine.

And then He left us, as He had told us He would. We were all gathered on the Mount of Olives together, and He was suddenly surrounded by a blinding light, becoming one with the light. I reached down and touched the hem of His garment as it glowed with radiance. Then He seemed to disappear before our eyes, into the mist, and He was gone.

This time there was no sorrow, for He had told us that He would not leave us alone. He would send a Comforter to us. We did not really understand what that meant, but we waited in patience in an upper room in Jerusalem. During this time, I revealed to the disciples the miracle of Jesus' birth and the appearances of the angel. I told them about the years before His baptism. The disciples chose another disciple from among the followers to take the place of Judas, who had betrayed Jesus. Matthias was chosen to complete the group of twelve.

Ten days after the Ascension, we were gathered in the upper room. We could hear the wind blowing, coming closer and closer. It swept into the room, filling the lungs of every person there, transforming them. Suddenly the disciples, all simple, plain-spoken men, were able to speak eloquently, filled with knowledge; and they were able to preach in languages not their own. Everyone who heard Peter speak that day heard the good news about Jesus in his own language. Many believed that day, becoming new followers of Jesus. At the beginning of the day, there were 120 of us. At the end of the day, nearly 3000 more had come to believe. It was a truly miraculous beginning.

———

After the coming of the Holy Spirit, the disciples had tremendous recall of all that Jesus had said during the three years of His ministry. Before, their minds and hearts had been closed, and they were not able to under-stand everything that He said. Now they were able to understand the deeper meaning of what He had taught. Some of what He taught only made sense in light of His resurrection.

In the early days, weeks, and months, they often spent much time talking about all that He had taught them. When they eventually went in their different directions to tell the world of Jesus, their teachings were the same. There was a consistency among the early church. There were still disagreements, but when there were, they attempted to meet together and discuss the issues among themselves to resolve them.

The disciples were given the gift of healing by the Holy Spirit. Solomon's Porch, near the Temple, was a favorite gathering place. People came from towns and villages surrounding Jerusalem to be healed by Peter and the other disciples and to hear them speak.

The Sadduces, who teach that there is no resur-rection of the dead, controlled the temple. They did not believe that Jesus had risen from the dead. They had

Peter and John arrested as they spoke at Solomon's Porch. Annas, the high priest, was surprised to hear them speak and defend themselves, for he knew that they were both uneducated men. Although it was obvious even to Annas that something had happened to them that had changed them, he did not want their teaching to continue. He released them, ordering them not to speak to anyone else about Jesus. This would have been as impossible for them as telling them to stop breathing, for telling the Good News about Jesus was now the entire purpose of their lives.

For a number of years, the disciples stayed in Judea, often near Jerusalem, for their primary focus continued to be the Jewish people. We did not believe at that time that this was a new religion, for we believe that Jesus is the fulfillment of the prophesies from our Scripture. Many Jewish people have come to believe because of the teachings of the disciples, including many Greek-speaking Jews from the countries around Judea; but for many others, their hearts and their minds have remained closed, and they do not believe.

—◦∞◦—

We have been a very close community, very supportive of each other. The faithful have come from all walks of life. Some are from very wealthy families, some from very poor ones. It does not matter. Everyone contributes what they can for the good of all. The wealthy often sell their possessions and open their homes for worship and for the poor. At the beginning, we would gather together for a daily meal, but as our numbers have grown so rapidly, that custom has frequently given way to weekly meals together. However, we still have a strong sense of community, which has helped to make us strong for the more difficult years.

Because we believe that Jesus is the Messiah that we were promised in the prophecies, we continued to observe the Sabbath of our Fathers. We would also gather in the evenings of the seventh day for prayers, hymns, psalms, and teaching by the apostles, usually meeting in the homes of our wealthier members. And we would gather to break bread together.

Before Jesus died, on His last night with His disciples, He gave them a very special gift, a very special blessing. He gave them a way to physically remember Him and to bring Him into their lives and into their bodies. At the Passover supper, He broke bread and poured wine for them to eat and drink, which He told them were His body and His blood. He asked that they do that to remember Him, and so it has continued, as He had requested. Over time, we began to celebrate our new faith on the Lord's Day, on the day of His Resurrection. As part of the service, we are given bread and wine. It has become a weekly symbol of our faith, and it gives us strength for the week ahead.

After Jesus had returned to His Father, I was so proud of the men He had chosen to tell the world about Him, about the Good News that He had revealed, that we can have everlasting life with our God; this too is a mystery. These men were not educated men. They were simple men, peasants, fishermen, a tax collector. Suddenly they had the gift of persuasive speech, of organization, of remarkable courage.

Many felt threatened and frightened by what they considered a new religion, and many of His followers were persecuted. Stephen was the first to be stoned. He was such a wonderful young man, one of the seven chosen by the apostles to help settle conflicts that were developing between the Aramaic and the Greek-speaking faithful in Jerusalem. For those who witnessed his death, it was a powerful moment for they knew that our Lord Jesus had come to him at the moment of his death, just as He had promised.

This was the beginning of the first wave of persecutions against us. The Jewish leaders were concerned because this new faith was spreading beyond Jerusalem, to Damascus and Antioch, and even further, for wherever our faithful traveled they could not help but tell others of the joy they had found in Jesus.

—◦◦◦—

One of the leaders in the persecution of Christians, as we eventually began to call ourselves, was a young man named Saul, whom we now call Paul. He was one of many miraculous conversions. We were all very suspicious of him when we first heard that he suddenly claimed to be one of us. He had been behind the torture and death of many, including the beloved Stephen. He had been so determined to persecute Christians that he had traveled as far as Damascus to look for them and bring them back to Jerusalem to be imprisoned. The apostles were naturally suspicious of his sudden conversion, which happened on the road to Damascus. People suspected him of attempting to become a spy among us. I think that he understood their hesitancy in immediately accepting him as one of them. He spent several years teaching and preaching that Jesus was the Messiah, but he did not go to Jersusalem to meet with the apostles during that time.

When Paul finally did go to Jerusalem, he met with Peter and John, as well as Barnabas, who had earlier gone to Antioch to spread the Faith. While he was in Jerusalem, he came to see me at John's home, where I was living. We talked quietly in the garden, and he told me the details of his sudden and miraculous conversion. In the end, his sincerity was overwhelming, his dedication to our Lord obvious to me. My doubts about him vanished and I gave him my blessing. I told Peter and John that he had been chosen by Jesus, just as they had been. I think they still had some reservations about him, but they asked Barnabas to take Paul along on his next journey to Antioch, to help with the new Church there. He has spent many years now traveling to distant lands, teaching the Good News about Jesus. He has come to visit me on occasion, when he is passing through Ephesus, and I am always pleased to see him, for he has become one of the great missionaries of our faith.

———⟨⟨⟨———

For a number of years I lived, along with Mary Magdalene, in John's home on Mt. Sion, near Jerusalem, taking care of his mother, Salome, who was ill. One day Mary Magdalene, who was an incredibly strong-willed and brave woman, told me that after much prayer and thought, she had decided that she wanted to expose the unjust treatment of Jesus to the Romans. She was determined to go to Rome and present her case against Pilate, Annas and Caiaphas to the Emperor Tiberias. Accompanied by several other brethren, she journeyed to Rome and presented a red egg to the Emperor, greeting him with the words, "Christ is Risen." She used the red egg to show the Emperor that the blood of Christ washed the world and made it clean. She broke the shell, which represented the tomb, and peeled it away to show that Jesus had overcome death.

During the years in Jerusalem, new followers often sought me out, and as I sat in the garden, they would sit at my feet and listen as I told them about their beloved Jesus. I would often go with them on short pilgrimages. I went with some to Bethlehem, where I looked for and found the small cave where Jesus had been born. My heart filled with joy when I remembered those first days after His birth. I would also take them to the places where He had suffered and died, as well as to the tomb where we had buried Him. I wept as I revisited these places, remembering the suffering that He had endured; but at the tomb my tears would become tears of joy, for once again I would be reminded that the Resurrection had changed everything.

——————

Most of the apostles stayed in Jerusalem for several years, for at that time the primary focus of their preaching was to the Jewish people. Even when they went on the first missionary trips, they tended to focus on the Hebrew and Greek Jews who lived in those areas. About ten years after the Resurrection, a new wave of persecutions began. James, John's brother, was arrested and killed, the first of the apostles to become a martyr. His death pleased the Jewish leaders, and Herod also had Peter arrested and put in prison. We were all very concerned for his safety, fearful that he too would be killed by Herod. We gathered in the home of Mary, mother of John Mark, to pray for James, who was now

with our Lord, and to pray for Peter. In the mid
prayers, we heard a knock on the door, and
servant girl, Rhoda, also one of the faithful, wer
who it was. When she heard the voice call out '
she ran back to tell us, so excited that she had fo
to open the door. Once inside, Peter told us tha
we were all in prayer, an angel had come into the
and freed him, in the midst of the sleeping guard
were all so grateful to have him back with us, f
loved him, and his strong leadership was so impo
to the growing church.

As the persecutions continued, the apostles beg
go beyond Jerusalem and the surrounding area. 1
cast lots to see where each of them would go to pr
the Good News. I asked that I also be given a missi
Although I was no longer young, I was healthy
strong. I wanted to share in the joy of telling oth
about Jesus. I began to make plans to travel to Iberia,
from Jerusalem. However, before I could leave, t
angel Gabriel appeared to me and told me that I shou
remain where I was. One day, he said, I would go to th

Macedonian peninsula, to Mount Athos, where I would help to convert many pagan souls. I was told that Iberia would be enlightened at another time, by another woman. I was disappointed at first, but I had learned long ago to trust in God.

Although it did not happen for many years, eventually the angel's words came true, and I found myself at Mount Athos. Barnabas had named Lazarus to be the bishop of Cyprus. It had been many years since I had seen Lazarus, and he wrote to me, telling me that he longed to see me again, for I had known him almost his entire life. He was unable to travel because of his duties as bishop, and so he sent a ship for John, several others, and myself. However, there was a terrible storm at sea, and our ship was thrown off it's course. We found ourselves off the coast of Macedonia, near Mount Athos. We rested from our terrible ordeal at sea, and I was overwhelmed by the beauty of the place. The inhabitants of the area were pagans, and I prayed for them. Over the years, I had learned to speak Greek adequately well, and so I told them about my Son,

about the message He had brought to the world; and they believed. I was filled with such spiritual joy that so many were having the opportunity to hear and to believe, and I continue to pray for the spiritual lives of all who live there.

———

Many of us have been martyred over the years. I fear even more widespread persecutions in the years ahead, for we are becoming more bold in our missions to tell people about Jesus, traveling farther and farther from Judea. With each wave of persecutions, the officials hope that they will crush us and that we will become discouraged and abandon our missionary efforts; but the opposite has become true. The more we suffer, the stronger we have become, strengthened by the Holy Spirit.

John and I fled from Jerusalem and went to Ephesus, where he continued his preaching. From there I sometimes traveled with him to other cities. The focus of the missionary efforts has been more and more to the Gentiles, for the apostles have come to realize that Jesus' message is for all who have the ears to hear and the desire to take Him into their hearts.

I have met so many wonderful and brave women as I have traveled with John. Women have been so responsive to the message that Jesus brought to the world. Often it has been the wives and mothers who have been the ones to lead entire families into our new faith, converting them through their own example.

Although these past years have been busy ones, Jesus has always been in my thoughts and in my heart. I have never felt lonely for Him, for I know that He is always with me, and that has been a comfort to me.

James and Jude, two of Joseph's sons have been faithful servants of our faith. James was named the first bishop of Jerusalem. Jude is a very humble man. He has always considered himself to be unworthy of being called "the brother of Jesus," and so he has always referred to himself as "the brother of James."

John has been as kind to me as if he were my own

son. His own mother died years ago, and since leaving Jerusalem, I have lived in his home here in Ephesus. The apostles often come to visit me on their way home from their travels. Many of the new followers come as well, those who had never met Jesus when He was with us. Luke, a Greek physician who travels with Paul, has come to visit with me several times. He and others are beginning to write down the life and teachings of Jesus while there are still eyewitnesses alive. He told me that Mark, who has traveled with Paul and Barnabas, is writing an account of Jesus' life. Luke is also interested in writing an account that will include His birth and childhood. I told him the story about my Son's birth and the mysterious circumstances surrounding it. I told him a bit about Jesus' childhood. Luke is also an artist, and one day he asked if I would sit for him so that he could paint my portrait. It is the only painting ever done of me. My eyes are weak now, so I have not seen it clearly. However, he was pleased that I had consented, and he seemed to think that it would be important for future generations.

—◦◦◦—

During these past years as I have had time to reflect on my life, I have often thought about growing up in the Temple. At the time it seemed a very normal life, for it was all that I knew. I now realize what an unusual childhood I had. Girls are usually educated at home and taught only the skills they will need to be good wives and mothers. Studying Scripture is considered unnecessary, even undesirable for girls, and yet I spent years reading Scripture, learning of our prophecies, and learning the inner prayer of the heart. In reflection, I've come to realize that from the beginning of my life, possibly even before, God had chosen me to be the mother of Jesus. However, my destiny was not sealed until I said "yes."

I think that God knew that I would be a better mother for His Son if I were well educated in the Scriptures and the prophecies. From the beginning I understood and accepted the enormous responsibility God had given to me, and I understood my role in all of this. Those years in the Temple have been invaluable. The Scriptures have brought me comfort, especially the beloved Psalms. The inner prayer of the heart has given me peace of mind and peace of soul. I was very blessed to have had a childhood that made me so spiritually strong.

Now that I am older, I take a less active roll in our community, preferring to spend most of my time here at home in my garden in Ephesus, tending my plants or just sitting quietly in the warm sunshine that eases this aching body. As I think back over the remarkable life I have lived, about the incredible gift I was given, I know that I have truly been blessed among women.

If future generations remember me, my role in these great events, I pray that they do not make me into something that I am not. I am not a goddess. I am a simple woman who became a mother. I am a simple woman who said to God, "Thy will be done."

I am getting older, and I can feel death hovering at the edges of my life. My sight is failing me, but I can still feel the warmth of the sun, smell the flowers, hear the birds. The face of my beloved Jesus is always so clear in my mind, and I know for a certainty deep within my soul that as my life departs, my Son and my Lord will be there. I pray that He will watch over you.

———✸———

And the angel came in unto her, and said, Hail, thou that art highly favored, the Lord is with thee: blessed art thou among women.

– Luke 1:28

Blessed art thou among women, and blessed is the fruit of thy womb.

– Luke 1:42

Rejoice, O Mother of God and maiden, Mary, full of grace, the Lord is with thee. Blessed art thou among women, and blessed is the fruit of thy womb, for thou hast given birth to the Savior of our souls.

– Orthodox Hymn

About the Author

Denise Sawyer is a native of Indiana, where she received a Masters Degree in Education from Indiana University. She has been a teacher, a Foreign Service wife, a mother, a folk artist, a secretary, and now a writer. She and her husband Roger have two sons, David and Michael. Denise and Roger now live in Virginia, along with their dog Timba.

Ordering Information

If you would like to order a copy of *My Name is Mary: The Story of the Mother of Jesus* or if you would like to be on our mailing list for upcoming books from Still Waters Publishers, please write to:

Still Waters Publishers
P.O. Box 403
Dunn Loring, VA 22027

Telephone orders: Call 1-866-204-4860 toll free. Please have your Visa or MasterCard ready.

On-line orders: Visit our website: www.stillwaterspublishers.com.

Postal orders: Send check or money order for $12.95 to Still Waters Publishers, P.O. Box 403, Dunn Loring, VA 22027 USA

Sales tax: Please add 4.5% for books shipped to Virginia addresses.

Shipping and handling:
Priority Mail: $4 for the first book, $2 for each additional book to the same address.
First Class: $3 for the first book, $1.50 for each additional book.
Book Rate: $2 for the first book, $1 for each additional book.